Well-known Tales from
PANCHATANTRA

Om
KIDZ
An imprint of Om Books International

Reprinted in 2017

An imprint of Om Books International

Corporate & Editorial Office
A 12, Sector 64, Noida 201 301
Uttar Pradesh, India
Phone: +91 120 477 4100
Email: editorial@ombooks.com
Website: www.ombooksinternational.com

Sales Office
107, Ansari Road, Darya Ganj,
New Delhi 110 002, India
Phone: +91 11 4000 9000
Fax: +91 11 2327 8091
Email: sales@ombooks.com
Website: www.ombooks.com

ISBN: 978-81-87107-87-3

Printed in India

Contents

The Intelligent Hare

Once upon a time, there was a dense forest,
which had lots of animals and birds living in
it. All the animals and birds lived together
happily. No animal or bird ever killed a smaller
one for food. However, there was one exception,

and that was the king of the jungle – an evil lion. The lion hunted around the forest at all times and killed the animals for food.

One day, the animals could not take it anymore. So they got together for a meeting. "It is not fair," said the bear. "He is killing so many of us, that one day this forest will not have any animals left."

So, all the animals, led by the elephant decided to talk to the king. "Your majesty," said the elephant, "You are killing so many of us, when you need only one for food!"

"We suggest you kill only one of us each day," said the clever fox.

The lion thought for a few minutes and said, "Fine! One of you will come to me each day

as food. The day you do not turn up, I will kill all of you." The animals agreed.

From that day, one animal would leave his family to go to the lion as food. This went on for many days, till one morning it was the hare's turn to go to the king. The intelligent hare was walking to the lion's den, when he saw a well on the way. Suddenly, a bright thought struck him, and he almost ran to the den.

Seeing him, the lion roared and said, "I was wondering where you were!" The hare replied, "Master, I was on my way to your den. But on my way, I was stopped by another lion who said he was the king of the jungle. He called you a fraud and wanted you to fight him to prove your supremacy."

The lion was livid with rage. He said, "Bring him here and I will teach him a lesson." But the hare managed to persuade the lion to go with him. He guided the lion to the well and asked him to look inside.

The foolish lion looked at his own reflection in the water and thinking it was his competitor, jumped inside. That was his end. All the animals rejoiced at the intelligence of the clever hare.

The Four Friends

In a forest lived three friends – turtle, crow and a little mouse. All day long, the friends would eat and play together. One day, while the friends were sitting near the lake, they saw a deer running for life.

Soon he came near the place where they were sitting, and fell down on the mud. He had fainted. The turtle sprinkled some water from the lake on him. In a

few minutes, the deer opened his eyes. He told the three friends that he was running for life from a hunter.

The crow flew right to the top of a large tree to check where the hunter

was. He came down and assured the deer that the hunter had caught some other animal, and was going back home.

From that day on, the deer joined the group of friends. Together, they lived happily, until one day the deer did not reach the usual place where the friends would meet.

The crow was worried and flew through the forest looking for him. He found the deer caught in a hunter's net. He flew right back

to where his friends were waiting, and told the mouse what had happened. The mouse scurried across the forest and found the deer. Slowly and steadily he cut through the net. Meanwhile, the animals saw the turtle walking towards them. The deer thought to

himself, "What lovely friends I have! All of them have come to help me in my time of need." Just when the deer was thinking about his friends, the crow alerted everyone about the hunter approaching. The mouse quickly

scurried into a hole. The crow was perched on top of a tree, and the deer got up and sprinted away. Finally, only the poor turtle was left behind.

The hunter picked up the turtle, strung him on his bow and walked away. A few minutes after the hunter had left the spot, the three friends got together and worked out a plan.

The hunter was walking along the lake, when he saw a dead deer lying on the path.

He put the turtle down, thinking it was his lucky day and walked across to the deer. When he was nearing the deer, the crow cawed and to the hunter's surprise, the deer got up and sprinted away.

The hunter could not believe his eyes. He turned around, and saw that the turtle he had tied to his bow was no longer there. The mouse had cut the strings while the hunter

had gone towards the deer and the turtle had slipped into the lake.

The poor hunter was left crying on the path with no catch, while the good friends happily thanked each other.

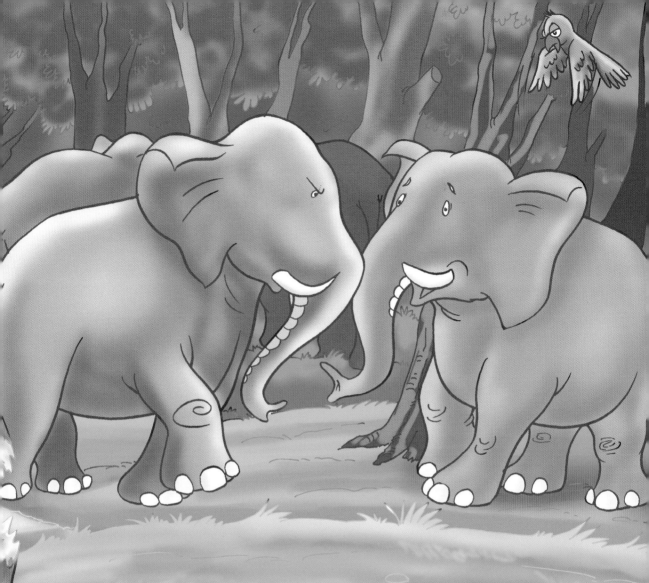

The Hare and the Elephant King

Long, long ago, the elephants ruled the jungle instead of the lion. They were big, strong and the mightiest of all.

Unfortunately, one hot summer, the water in the forest dried up. The animals started dying one by one. The elephant king was worried. He had to save the animals. He had heard about

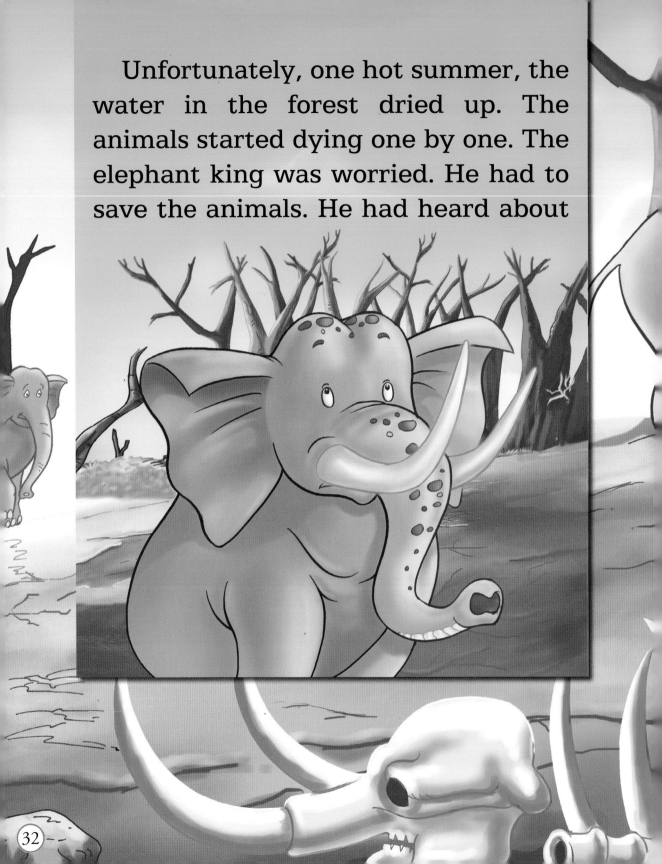

another forest which had a huge lake. It was not too far away from where they lived. The elephant, along with all the animals, went in search of the lake. After many days and nights of travel, the animals finally found the lake. They were full of joy seeing water after so many days, and rushed into the lake. Then they decided that they would come to the lake every day.

But, in their joy, they did not see that they were trampling across a colony of hares, which was living in that forest for ages. The hares were getting hurt. The trampling of the animals was happening every day.

So, one day, after the animals had left the lake, the hares got together to work out a plan, to save their lives. Their leader was sent to the elephant king to discuss the matter with him.

The hare told the elephant king, "Your majesty! I come from the land of the moon, who is our king. He is the owner of the lake and forbids you or your subjects to drink from it. So

I request you to find another lake." The elephant replied, "Take me to your king. I would like to meet him." The clever hare took the elephant to the lake during the night and pointed to the reflection of the shining moon in the water.

He said, "Look how our king is shaking with anger at you!" The elephant saw the moon shivering in the water, and assumed that what the hare was saying was true.

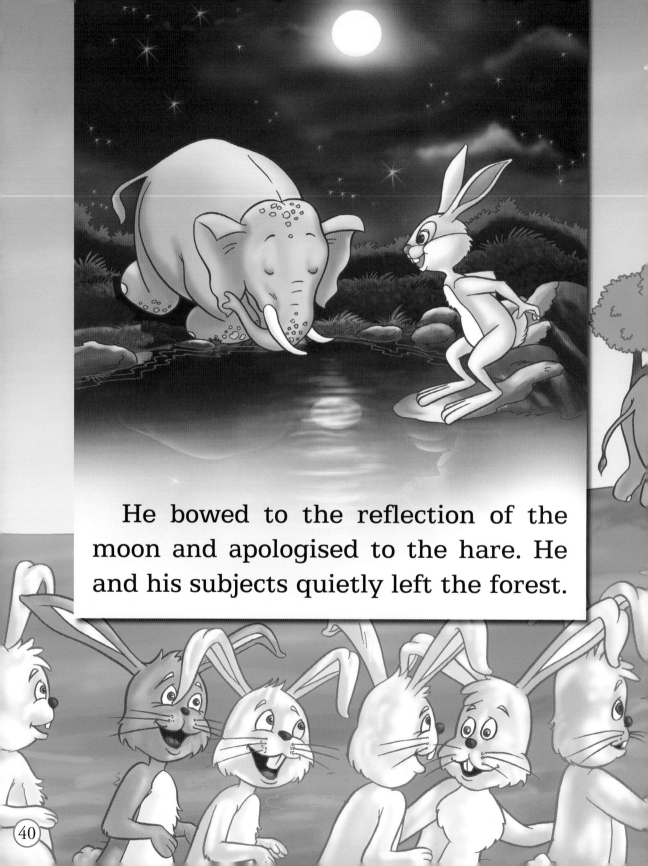

He bowed to the reflection of the moon and apologised to the hare. He and his subjects quietly left the forest.

The animals never returned to the lake. Thus, the hare saved his entire colony with his bravery and quick thinking.

The Jackal's Quick Thinking

One day, a jackal found a dead elephant and was very happy that he had found food for many days.

But unfortunately, the elephant's hide was too thick to bite into. The jackal was wondering what he would do, when he saw a lion approaching.

He saluted the lion and said, "Oh great king! This humble gift lying in front of you is my offering to you." The lion replied, "I do not take what is killed by others. So consider this as my gift to you."

Saying so, the lion walked away. A few minutes later, a tiger crossed the same path. The jackal knew that he would have to use some quick thinking. So he said, "My lord! Please pass by quickly. I am guarding this

elephant, which was killed by the mighty
lion himself. The lion has vowed to kill any
tiger that he sees; as a tiger had once tried
to eat an elephant that the lion had killed. So

your life is in grave danger!" The tiger thanked the jackal for warning him and ran for his life.

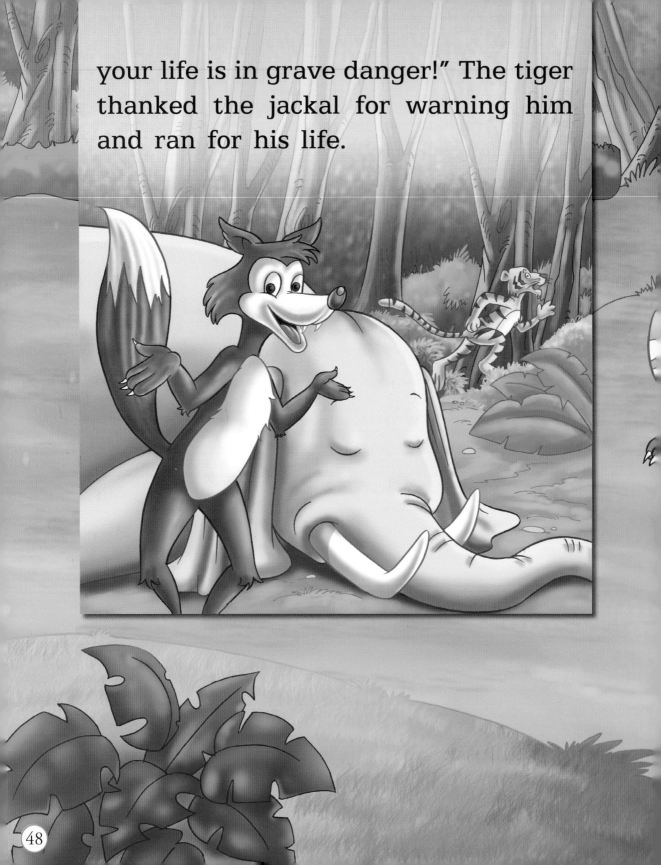

Just when the jackal was getting impatient
about finding someone to bite into the
elephant's hide, he saw a leopard. He knew
he could use the leopard's sharp teeth to solve
his problem. So he told the leopard, "Oh great

leopard! I am guarding the elephant, while the lion who killed it, has gone for a bath. Please feast yourself on it before he returns."

The leopard replied, "I would be mad to do that, for the lion would kill me!" To that the

cunning jackal said, "Do not worry! You can feast on it till he returns. I will signal you when I see him coming." The jackal waited for the leopard to bite into the hide and then signalled the lion's arrival. The leopard ran away in fear.

The jackal sat down to enjoy his catch when he spotted another hungry jackal coming his way. Without wasting any time, he jumped on to that jackal, and beat him to a pulp in a bitter fight.

Finally, the victorious jackal sat down to enjoy the feast he had worked so hard for!

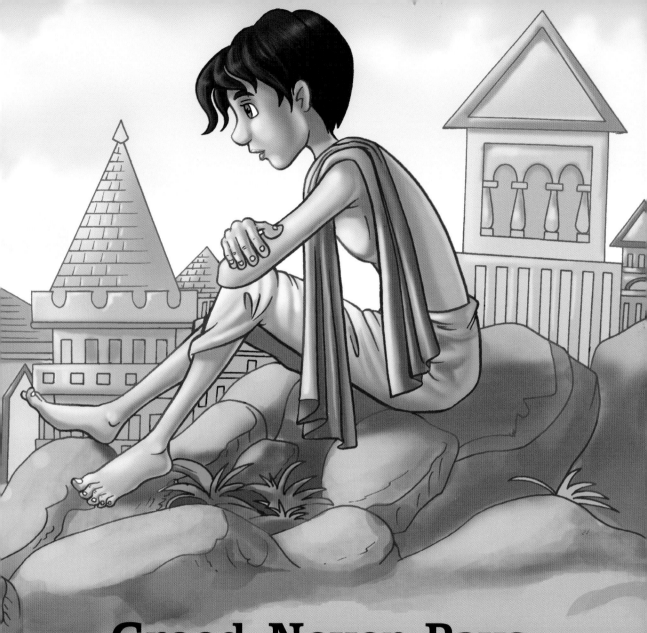

Greed Never Pays

In a small town, lived four young boys. They were so poor that they decided to leave their town and travel to earn money.

They took a dip in a river nearby and when they came out of the water after offering their prayers, a sage greeted them. The boys narrated their suffering to the sage, who took

pity on them and gave them four pearls. He told them, "I am giving you four pearls – one for each one of you. Travel to the mountains and stop when a pearl slips from your hand. You are sure to find a treasure there."

The boys left for the mountains in search for treasure. They were just a quarter way up the mountain range, when a pearl slipped out of a boy's hand. All of them stopped, and dug up the spot excitedly. They found copper at the end of their digging. The boy was very happy and decided to go back home with copper. But the other three felt that they needed to find gold.

They travelled for a few more days, when a pearl slipped out of another boy's hand. On digging up the place, they found silver. The

boy decided to pack the silver and head for his little town, while the other two decided to travel ahead in their search for gold.

They travelled across rough mountains, when another pearl slipped and fell at a spot. The boys dug up the spot and finally, there it was ... shining gold!

One of the two boys said, "Look! We have finally found what we were looking for. Let us take it and go home." To that, the other boy replied, "Think about it, every step we

have taken ahead has given better results – first it was copper, then it was silver and now it is gold. I am sure there must be something more precious than gold ahead."

Saying so, the boy decided to go ahead, while the one who found gold, could only shake his head in disapproval at his friend's greed.

So three boys had gone home with their treasures, and the fourth boy travelled for

days and finally, he came across a spot where there was a man standing with a wheel spinning on top of his head. The boy asked, "Who are you and why is this wheel spinning on your head?"

The moment the boy uttered these words, the wheel shifted from the man's head to the boy's head. The wheel caused a lot of pain, and the boy looked at the man in disbelief and cried, "Take this thing off my head!"

The man replied, "No one can remove the wheel. You will be saved from this pain when another boy like you comes to this spot in search of wealth and asks the same question you just asked. The magic of this wheel is that

you will not feel any hunger or thirst. But you will only feel the pain that greed causes."

The man left, while the boy stood there repenting at how his greed had brought him such misfortune.

The Crane and the Crab

Once upon a time, in a lake lived an old crane. He was so old that it was becoming very difficult for him to hunt for food. One day, he was standing on a rock crying, when a crab came to him and asked, "Uncle, what has made you so unhappy?"

The smart crane realised the opportunity. He replied, "I now repent for my sins of eating the fish in this lake during all these years."

The crab was surprised. He asked, "What makes you think like this?"

The crane replied, "I have heard that a dark future awaits these fish. It is said that there will be no rain in the coming years and the lake will dry up. So, all the fish you are seeing today will die one by one. Soon there will be none left in the lake."

The crab asked the crane for a solution and sure enough, the crane offered to help the fish by carrying them one by one to a bigger lake. Just as the crane had expected, the crab went and talked to all the fish. The innocent fish trusted the crane, who carried one fish every day in his beak. He would go a distance

and then smash the unsuspecting fish against a rock, kill it and eat it.

For days, the crane feasted on one fish after the other, until it was the crab's turn. The crab had been waiting for his chance with great excitement.

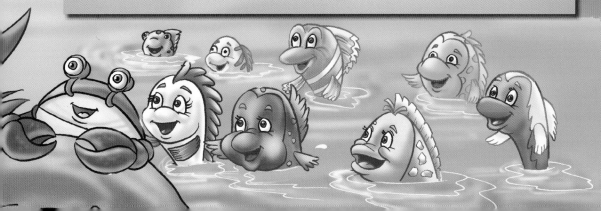

He told the crane, "Uncle, it is finally my turn to go and swim in the water of the new lake."

The crane carried the crab on his back and flew the distance he always did. Suddenly the crab saw piles of

fish bones lying at a distance. He quickly realised what the crane had been doing for so long. He asked the crane, "Uncle, why do I see so many bones lying around?" The crane replied, "You have been foolish to trust me. Now you will die the same way as your fish friends did."

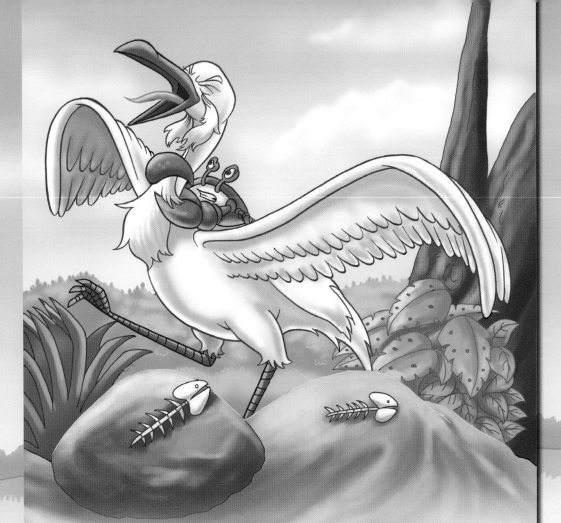

The crab was quick to answer. He asked, "Is it?" And before the crane could react, he had bitten the crane's neck to death.

He then took the neck back to the lake where the other fish were waiting for the crane to come back and take them. He told the fish, "From now on, we have learnt not to trust anyone so quickly."

The remaining fish rejoiced at the crab's quick thinking, which had saved their lives.

OTHER TITLES IN THIS SERIES

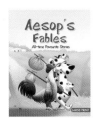     

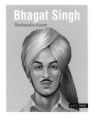 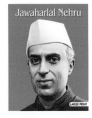 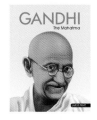   

 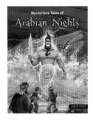  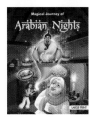 

FASCINATING TALES FROM
PANCHATANTRA

An imprint of Om Books International

Reprinted in 2017

Om
KIDZ

An imprint of Om Books International

Corporate & Editorial Office
A-12, Sector 64, Noida 201 301
Uttar Pradesh, India
Phone: +91 120 477 4100
Email: editorial@ombooks.com
Website: www.ombooksinternational.com

Sales Office
107, Ansari Road, Darya Ganj,
New Delhi 110 002, India
Phone: +91 11 4000 9000
Fax: +91 11 2327 8091
Email: sales@ombooks.com
Website: www.ombooks.com

ISBN: 978-81-87107-88-0

Printed in India

10 9 8 7

Contents

The Blue Jackal

It was a lonely, silent night. All the streets were empty. But, one could hear the cry of a jackal who was running for his life.

The jackal was trying to escape the hungry dogs, who were after him, on the streets of a small village.

The jackal was almost at his last breath, when he saw the open door of a washerman's house. He ran into the house and tried to find a place to hide. He jumped into a tub that was lying there, but in the darkness could not see that it had blue dye in it.

A few minutes later, the jackal came out of his hiding place. Little did he know the change in his colour, till he saw the same dogs, who were chasing him, running away in fright.

The jackal breathed a sigh of relief and walked to the forest.

But, when the animals saw him, all of them were terrified. "What is that strange creature?"

asked the elephant. "I have never seen an animal of this colour," said the panther.

"It has come from another land," hissed the snake. "Must be powerful!" hooted the owl.

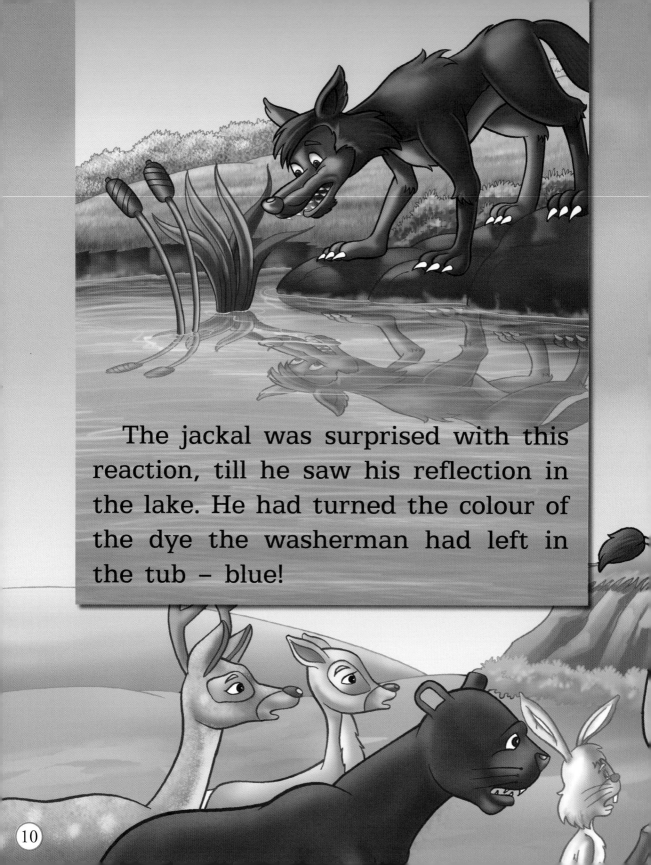

The jackal was surprised with this reaction, till he saw his reflection in the lake. He had turned the colour of the dye the washerman had left in the tub – blue!

The clever jackal thought he could now use his new colour to trick the animals. He proclaimed himself the king of the forest, and began his rule. He appointed the lion as his minister, the wolf as his assistant and the

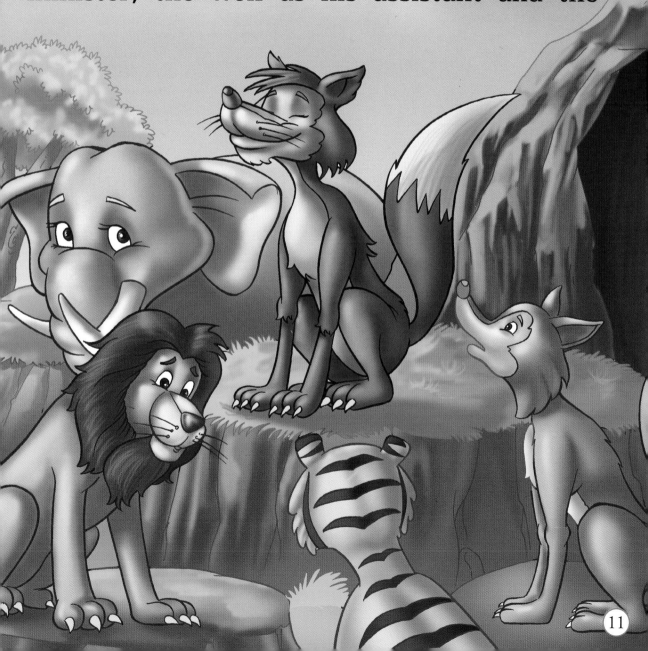

tiger as his hunter. Everyday the tiger would hunt for food and bring the kill to the new king as food.

The jackal had ordered all the other jackals to leave the forest. His life was just perfect. He had all the mighty animals looking after his every need.

One night, he was resting in the den, when he heard the cry of another jackal. Since crying out in the night was his nature, he cried back.

The animals outside his den were shocked to hear their mighty king crying out like a jackal. They peeped inside the den and realised that the new king was indeed a jackal – only

in a different colour. They jumped on him at once and gave him a nice beating as punishment!

That was the end of the jackal's reign as the king of the forest.

The Elephant's Punishment

Two sparrows lived happily in their little nest on a mango tree. One day, the female sparrow laid eggs in her nest, which she and her husband guarded closely.

One morning, an elephant came to the tree
seeking shelter from the hot sun. It was so
hot that the angry elephant tore a branch off
the tree. Sadly, that was the branch on which
the nest was.

The female sparrow cried and cried. Her eggs got crushed in front of her. She promised herself that she would teach the evil elephant a lesson. The elephant did not know about the harm he had caused, but he had taken away the lives of her children!

So she flew to her friend, the woodpecker for help. The woodpecker said, "Do not worry my friend! A friend in need is a friend indeed. I will seek help from my friend the fly, and together, we will punish the elephant."

The woodpecker and the sparrow flew to the fly. The fly said, "Let us plan what to do with the help of my friend, the wise frog who lives in the pond." All the three went to the wise frog.

The frog said, "My friends, you will not be disappointed. My perfect plan is sure to teach the elephant a lesson."

The next day, the elephant was walking along the forest when he heard a lovely tune. It was the fly humming in his ears. It was so sweet that the elephant closed his eyes, enjoying the melody.

The moment he closed his eyes, the woodpecker swooped down from a nearby branch and poked all around his face! "Oooooo!" the elephant howled with pain. His face was hurting where the woodpecker had poked and scratched and the heat was making it worse!

He decided to splash some water on his face to relieve him of the pain. But where was the water? He could not see, as his eyes were shut tight with the pain.

Suddenly, he heard a frog croaking. He followed the croaking for a while.

All of a sudden, the elephant felt something was pulling him down. He realised that he had stepped into the huge smelly marshes!

"Oh no!" cried the elephant. "This is getting worse...what an awful smell and I can't even see anything!" He tossed around splashing in

the mud and dead plants. His giant body was tangled in the weeds and he was fighting to get out. "The frog

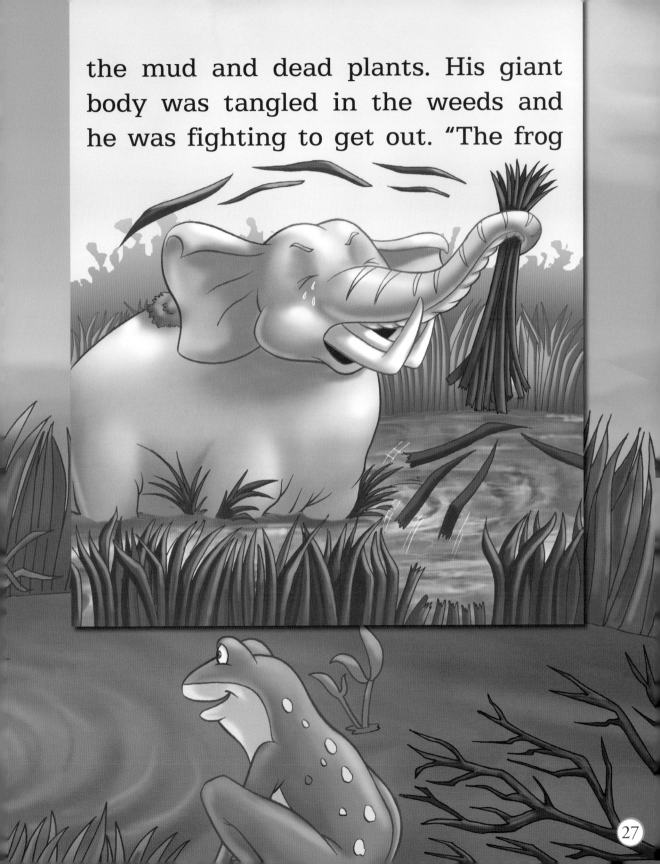

has cheated me... what harm could have I done to him?" wondered the elephant. "Please help me frog!" he cried, "why are you troubling me so?"

"You destroyed the sparrow's nest and broke all her eggs ... that is why, the sparrow, the fly and I decided to punish you," said the wise frog.

The elephant fell down tired. He was truly sorry for what he had done and decided never to act in anger again.

The Mouse-Girl and the Sage

There was a sage living in his little hut in the forest. Every morning he would go to the river to offer his prayers to the Sun God.

One morning, while he was praying—his palms open and outstretched—he felt something dropping into them. When he opened his eyes, he saw a tiny mouse!

The mouse was scared that the sage would drop her into the water. But the kind sage carried the mouse to safety and asked her what had happened.

The mouse said, "I was walking in the forest when an eagle swooped upon me and

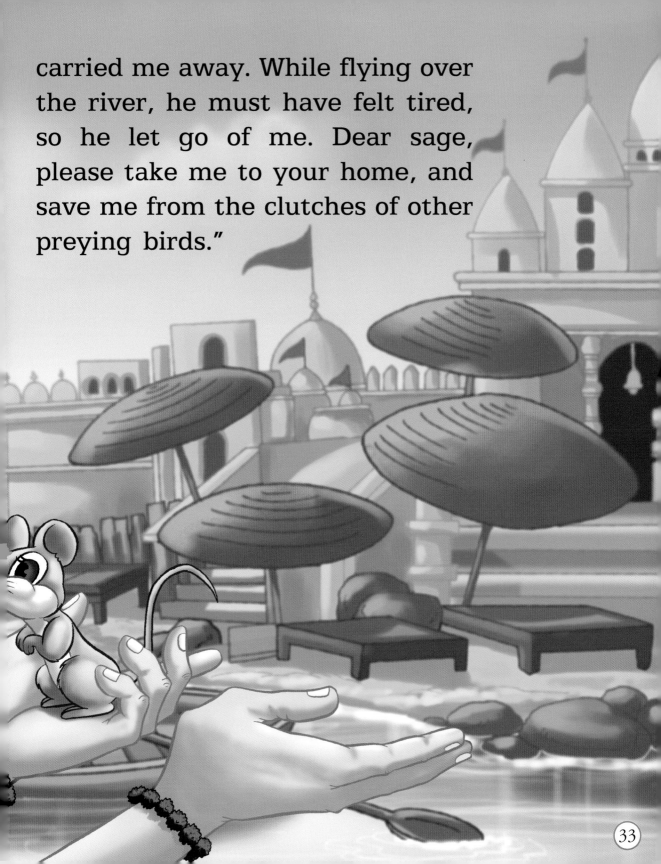

carried me away. While flying over the river, he must have felt tired, so he let go of me. Dear sage, please take me to your home, and save me from the clutches of other preying birds."

The sage thought for a second, and then with his magical powers turned the mouse into a beautiful girl child. He took the girl to his hut as he had no children. For years, the lovely girl was loved and looked after by the sage and his wife.

Many years passed and it was time for the girl to get married. The sage asked the girl whom she wanted to marry. The mouse in the form of the girl said, "I want to marry the mightiest person in the universe." The sage took her to the Sun God. The girl asked the

Sun God, "Are you the mightiest?" The Sun smiled and said, "I am mighty, but not the mightiest. The God of the Clouds is mightier than me. He can hide me whenever he feels like it."

So the sage and the girl went to the God of the Clouds. But he said, "The God of the Winds is mightier than me. He can push me around wherever he wants."

When the sage and the girl went to meet the God of the Winds, he said, "The God of the Mountains is mightier than me. He is so big that he can stop me whenever he wants."

Finally, the sage went to meet the God of the Mountains. But he gave them a surprising answer. He said, "Oh holy sage!

I am mighty. But a tiny creature like the mouse can dig a hole in me. So I believe that the King of the Mice is the mightiest."

Hearing this, the girl was very happy. After all, she was a mouse herself!

So the sage changed her back into a mouse, and married her to the King of the Mice, and they lived happily ever after.

The Clever Servant

Mir was a servant who worked in the King's castle. One day, it was the wedding of a rich merchant's daughter.

Mir decided to attend the wedding. When he reached the merchant's house, he sat on one of the chairs that had been kept for the rich people of the kingdom.

When the merchant saw this, he rushed to Mir, and rudely asked him to get off the chair.

Mir was insulted and was very angry. He thought of a plan to avenge this terrible insult.

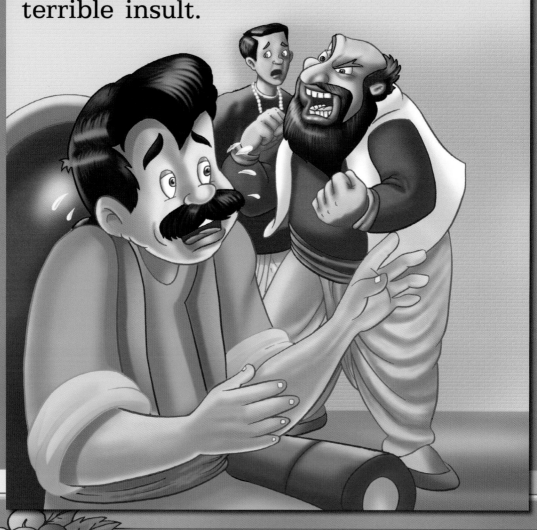

The next day while he was at work at the King's castle, he started muttering loudly, knowing well that the King was walking towards him. He said, "Oh what a wife the King has! She spends more of her time at the merchant's house rather than her own!"

The King was shocked to hear Mir saying this. He held Mir by the arm and shouted in anger, "Can you prove what you are saying? You are insulting the Queen and me by saying such things!"

Mir replied, "Sir, I don't know what I was saying. I had too much to drink last night, and must have muttered something. Please pardon me for it."

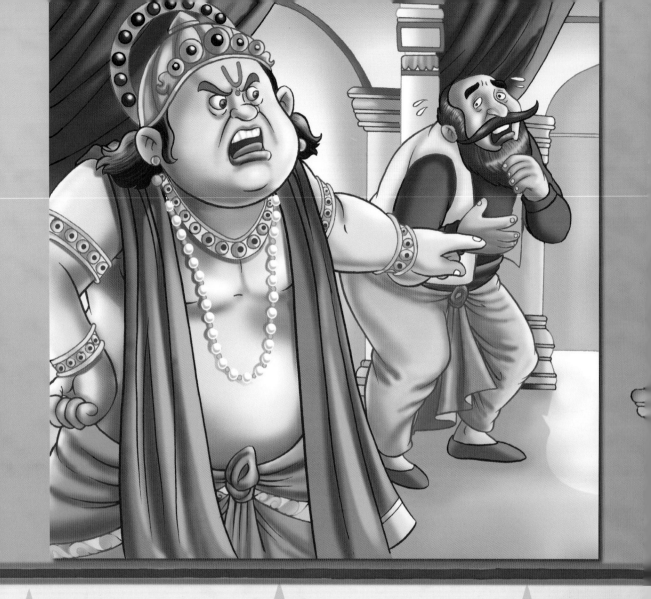

But the seed of doubt had been planted in the King's mind.

He immediately stopped all the grants he had given to the merchant, and threw him out of the position he held at the King's court. The merchant could not understand why the King had suddenly become so angry with him.

He decided to seek an audience with the King and discuss the problem. But the King's guards would not allow him inside.

Luckily for him, Mir was passing by. Seeing that the merchant was in difficulty, Mir went up to the guards and said loudly, "Don't you know that he is the kingdom's richest merchant and a very respectable man?"

Hearing Mir's words, the guards allowed the merchant to enter.

When the merchant returned home, he realised how unfair he had been to Mir at his daughter's wedding. So he went back to the

castle the next morning and apologised to Mir. He invited him home and gifted him with a bag of silver coins.

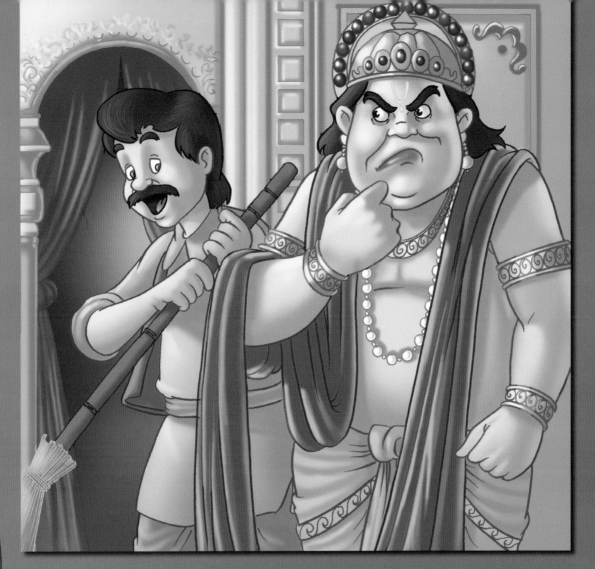

Mir now decided to reverse the harm he had caused to the merchant. So the next day while he was at work at the castle, he again started muttering loudly seeing the King walking towards him. He said, "What a foolish King this kingdom has! He eats fruits in the washroom!"

The King was shocked with what he heard. Then he thought to himself, "If Mir could say this about me in his drunken state, he must have been lying about the merchant and the Queen a few days ago."

The King realised that he had acted in haste, and invited the merchant to the castle to make amends.

United, You Always Win

On the top of a large banyan tree lived a crow. Every morning, the crow would fly to the village to gather food and would come back by night.

One day, the crow was flying to the village, when he saw a hunter approaching the tree with seeds in his hand.

The crow thought to himself, "This hunter is out to kill someone! The grains in his hand are to tempt the birds."

So the crow flew back to the tree and gathered all the other animals and birds living in the tree, "Friends, there is an evil hunter coming towards our home. He has some delicious grains in his hand. He will throw them around to tempt you. Do not touch any of them or your life will be in danger."

Just as the crow had warned, the hunter threw the grains in front of the tree. None of the birds or animals went near it.

Alas! From the sky descended a flock of hundred pigeons to eat the grains. The pigeons pounced on the grains, and before they knew it, the hunter had cast his net on them.

All the pigeons were trapped. They cried out to their king, "It was a trap! The evil hunter will now kill all of us."

The king said, "Do not worry! I have a plan. But we will all have to work together for the plan to succeed."

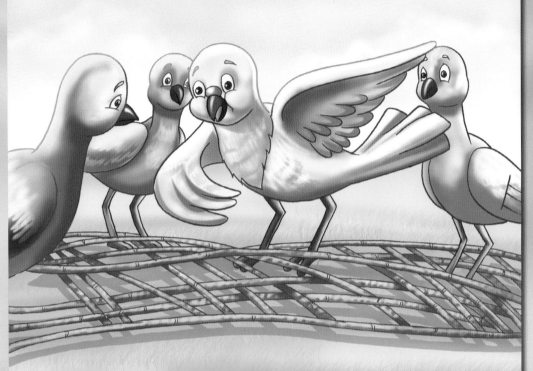

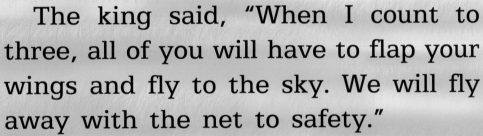

The king said, "When I count to three, all of you will have to flap your wings and fly to the sky. We will fly away with the net to safety."

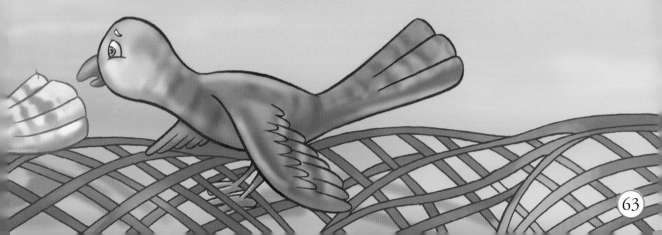

As the hunter was walking towards the net, he was thinking how lucky he was to trap so many birds in one day. But he was in for a big surprise!

The birds flapped their wings and rose to the sky right in front of his eyes.

The hunter cried out, "Wait, wait, you are taking my net with you …"

But the birds had flown too far away and there was nothing the hunter could do. When they were safely away from the hunter, the

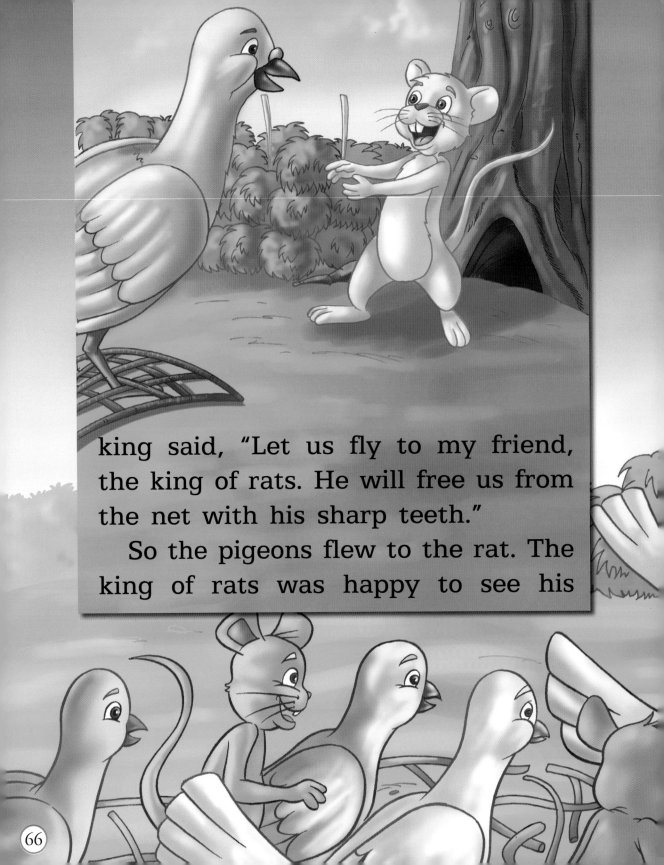

king said, "Let us fly to my friend, the king of rats. He will free us from the net with his sharp teeth."

So the pigeons flew to the rat. The king of rats was happy to see his friend, though in a net! He called all his friends and within minutes the pigeons were free.

The king of rats looked at the free pigeons and said, "When you are united, you can do anything you want!"

The Dead Lion

Four young boys were on their way home from their school. They had spent many years in learning all the scriptures and other special powers from their learned teacher.

But one of the boys, whose name was
Gorukhi, had more of common-sense than
knowledge. So, the other three would
tease him all through the day. Gorukhi
was very unhappy hearing their words,
but could not do a thing.

On their way home, the boys came across a huge heap of bones lying on the road. The boys wondered what the heap was.

One of the boys said, "This could be our chance to test our knowledge. Let us put the

bones and flesh together to find out what animal this could be."

The other two boys readily agreed, while Gorukhi was not so sure. He felt doing such a thing may not be safe. He knew an animal with such big bones would surely be a frightful one.

He said, "I feel that we will be in danger trying to breathe life into such a big animal." The others snapped immediately, "Who is asking you? Step aside and see what your learned friends can do!"

The first boy said, "Watch as I put the bones together and make them into a skeleton with my powers." Soon the skeleton took shape.

The second boy said, "I will now use my powers to put flesh and blood on to the skeleton."

Right in front of their eyes, the bones and flesh turned into an animal that everyone recognised. It was a lion! Everyone except Gorukhi was very happy. They exclaimed, "All these years of learning have not gone waste. We could actually create a lion from just bones!"

The third boy said proudly, "My friends! What is a mass of flesh without life in it? Watch as I breathe life into the lion."

Gorukhi was alarmed. He asked, "What are you doing? If you breathe life into the lion, he will eat us all up. Do not do it my friend!"

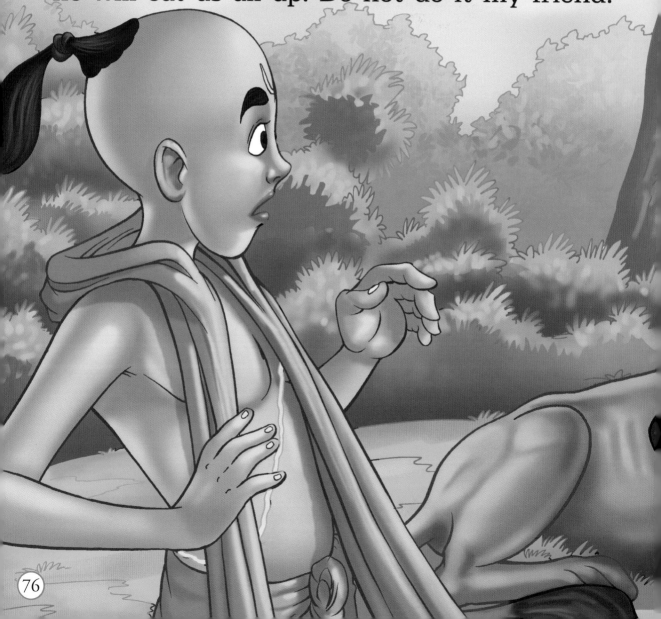

But the third boy was angry at Gorukhi's advice. He asked, "When these two have shown how talented they are, are you suggesting that I miss out on my chance to show my skills?"

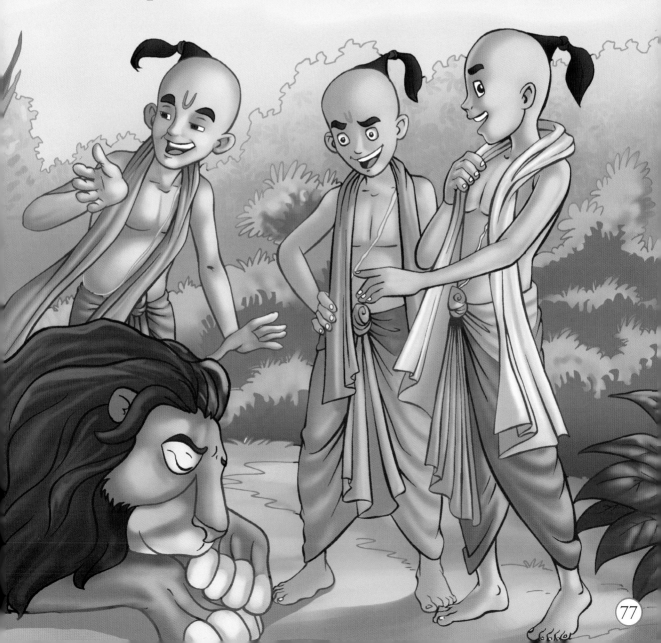

Gorukhi was sad that his learned friends lacked the power to see what was in store for them when the lion would come to life. So he decided to save his life and climbed up a tree.

Lo and behold! The third boy breathed life into the lion. For a second, the lion opened his eyes and looked at the three boys standing in front of him. In the next second, he pounced on them and killed them all!

Gorukhi sat on the branch of the tree watching how his friends lost their lives, because they had all the learning, but no common-sense.

OTHER TITLES IN THIS SERIES

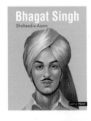  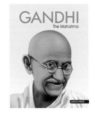   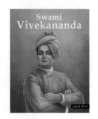

 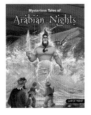  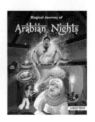